THE PURPLE SLUGGY WORRY WARTS

BOOKS IN THE QUENTIN QUIRK'S MAGIC WORKS SERIES

Attack of the Bum-Biting Sharks

The Purple Sluggy Worry Warts

Coming soon

Gooey Green Bogey Blobs

Revenge of the Boy-Eating Snake

QUENTIN QUIRK'S MAGIC WORKS

THE PURPLE SLUGGY WORRY WARTS

MATT KAIN

ILLUSTRATED BY
JIM FIELD

MACMILLAN CHILDREN'S BOOKS

For Xav and Max – MK

For Mum and Dad - JF

First published 2009 by Macmillan Children's Books
a division of Macmillan Publishers Limited
20 New Wharf Road, London N1 9RR
Basingstoke and Oxford
Associated companies throughout the world
www.panmacmillan.com

ISBN 978-0-330-51022-6

1 3 5 7 9 8 6 4 2

A CIP catalogue record for this book is available from the British Library.

Printed and bound in the UK by CPI Mackays, Chatham ME5 8TD

CONTENTS

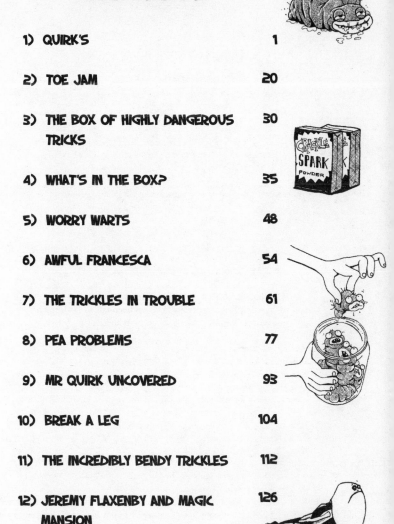

CHAPTER ONE
QUIRK'S

Jez and Charlie raced along Bleak Street then dropped their Beemos on to the pavement outside Quirk's. Jez took a deep breath, then knocked on the crumbling oak door.

A few seconds later, it opened a tiny crack and Mr Quirk's spindly nose stuck out. The thick yellow nails of his knobbly fingers curled around the wood. 'My drear boys,' he snarled. 'Horrified to see you. Go away.'

'Mr Quirk, please let us in!' called Jez. 'We need your help!'

'Huh!' scoffed Mr Quirk. 'I think NOT!

I'm never letting you sticky revolting brats into my precious emporium again! Especially not after last time, when, if you recall, you ended up setting mini-sharks loose in the town's toilet system. Good. Bye.'

The door slammed shut. Mr Quirk was being his usual self, i.e. tall, bony and bad-tempered.

'Nothing'll go wrong this time, I promise,' called Jez through the keyhole. 'We just want to buy another trick.'

'No!'

'We've got money.'

Mr Quirk opened the door a fraction and sniffed the air. His long nose quivered. 'You stink,' he observed.

'Charming!' huffed Jez. 'I had a bath just last . . .' he paused, 'week,' he admitted.

Mr Quirk frowned (even more). 'I mean, apart from the general stench of grubby child. You also smell like a very ripe mouldy cheese, which, to the trained nose, is the highly distinctive stink of money. Come in then,' he snapped. 'But don't you dare touch ANYTHING or I'll be treating you both to some Extra-Strength Fingernail Remover.'

'Erm, don't you mean fingernail *polish* remover?' asked Charlie.

Mr Quirk gave him a wicked look. 'No, I don't,' he muttered darkly.

Jez gulped, and Charlie shoved his hands deep into his pockets.

Hearts pounding, Jez and Charlie stepped into the shop. The rows and rows of dusty old bottles and jars in all shapes and sizes were still the same. The green leather surface of Mr Quirk's wooden desk was still covered in bills and papers. The latest copy of *Magic Monthly* magazine was still open on the desk, showing an advertisement for the emporium.

The huge, dirty flagstones were also as cold as ever underfoot. Charlie shivered and scuffed his baseball boots nervously.

'Now, what exactly do you require?' asked Mr Quirk impatiently.

'Oh, anything really,' said Jez. 'A trick to play on my sister, Francesca, would be fun. She's being even more vile than usual, if that's possible.' He peered at one of the thick glass bottles. '"Big Beard Elixir",' he read. 'Now that sounds promising. Or how about one of these Most Alarming Ghost Alarm Clocks? That would put the wind up her!'

Mr Quirk looked outraged and snatched the clock. 'I am most certainly *not* selling you any more tricks after what happened last time!'

Charlie jumped, but Jez wasn't even listening. 'And, hey, wow, look at this!' he cried.

He had crossed the emporium and was heaving at the lid of a huge glass display case. Charlie gasped, remembering the threat of the Extra-Strength Fingernail Remover. He wondered why Jez didn't worry about things like that. You know, little things like *mortal danger*. There was one single item inside the case: a box. It was slightly bigger than a shoebox, and there were red, green and purple stripes painted on it. Its label read:

BOX OF HIGHLY
DANGEROUS
TRICKS

'I forbid you to open that case!' Mr Quirk screeched. His ancient knees creaked as he hurtled across the emporium and threw himself at the display case, knocking Jez out of the way. 'Get your snotty, greasy child-fingers away from there! That box is my most prized possession!' He glared at Jez, his dark eyes spitting fire.

If looks could kill, Jez would have keeled over on to the cold stone floor, stone cold dead. Instead he asked, 'What's in it?'

'I am certainly not telling *you*!' snapped Mr Quirk.

'It's probably things like fart powder and blue tongue sweets,' Jez guessed, 'but, you know, highly dangerous ones that blow your bum off or make your tongue stretch out and tie into a knot. Maybe there's even something as good as the bum-biting sharks in there, or a trick that makes you fly up in the air and stick to the ceiling by your little toe.' He sighed dreamily. 'A whole box of tricks, Charlie! *Highly dangerous* ones! Look out, Francesca – here we come!'

Charlie looked at the striped box in the display case. He used to have qualms about using magic on Francesca, but since she'd tipped him into a rotten slimy wheelie bin and sent him trundling down a steep hill towards a busy road . . . well, since then, the gloves were pretty much off. 'How much is it?' he asked.

'It doesn't matter how much it is,' sneered Mr Quirk, 'because I would never sell it to the likes of you. Besides, I know you don't *have* twenty pounds. You don't smell anywhere near mouldy-cheesy enough.'

Jez and Charlie exchanged a disappointed glance. Mr Quirk was right. Even if they could convince him to sell the box to them, where on earth were they going to get twenty quid from?

Mr Quirk's crackly voice cut into their thoughts. 'Right, come on, buy something then,' he snapped.

'Erm, I don't think we will, th-thanks,' said Jez, his voice trembling as Mr Quirk strode towards him. There was a wicked glint in his eye, and his arms were out-stretched in the strangling position

'Not buy anything!' he cried, fingers

twitching. 'What do you mean, not *buy* anything? When you have taken up so much of my valuable time?'

Jez backed towards the door.

'OK, w-w-we'll buy something,' Charlie stammered. He rummaged in his pockets and Jez did the same. Among the sweet wrappers and bus tickets and Subbuteo men they found a few coins. Jez handed his to Charlie, who fumbled nervously as he

counted up. 'We've got two pounds, forty-one pence,' he stammered, hoping it would be enough for something – anything.

Mr Quirk stalked over to a small table on which stood a number of glass jars. The sign on the table read:

'Char!' Jez hissed. 'That's our only money. We don't even know what Worry Warts are!'

'Jez, were you planning to leave this shop with *all* your fingernails?' asked Charlie flatly.

Jez gulped. 'I get your point. Worry Warts it is.'

The boys hurried over to the table and peered into the jars.

'But they're empty,' murmured Jez. He wondered if it was a trick. Mr Quirk was quite capable of taking their money in exchange for a jar of thin air.

'Well, of course they're empty, you nincompoop,' snapped Mr Quirk. 'Worry warts are no good unless they're harvested on the day of purchase. Follow me.'

Jez and Charlie stared at each other as Mr Quirk swept off across the shop. They were both thinking the same thing. *Harvested?* What on earth did that mean?

They followed Mr Quirk to a cabinet of glass bottles, where he counted three shelves down and six bottles to the right, until he reached the jar labelled Red Herrings. He gave it three sharp taps and the whole cabinet swung backwards. Jez and Charlie grinned at each other – they couldn't believe their luck. Once again, they were being let into the Magic Works – the secret back room where all Mr Quirk's magical inventions and potions were made.

Inside the room strange machines whirred and clicked, foul-smelling liquids spluttered and bubbled in large pots, and rows of test tubes sat on a long wooden bench, streaming brightly coloured smoke and fizzing to themselves. There was a tank of mini man-eating sharks for making Liquid Frighteners, something called a Spook-o-meter and, for some reason, a pile of smelly, holey old socks heaped in a corner.

Mr Quirk ushered them over to the far wall, opened a creaky cupboard door and stepped inside. 'Hurry up!' he hissed. 'They can't be exposed to light, you know, not while they're still growing.' He grabbed their arms, yanked them into the cupboard and shut the door.

Then Mr Quirk flicked on an ultraviolet light. A purple glow filled the tiny space.

Charlie and Jez stared around them. 'Err! Yuck!' they cried. But they didn't say anything else after that. They were too busy trying to hold their breath because the humid air smelt like a pungent combination of sweaty trainer and dead rat. On every wall was some kind of slimy yellow substance, on which were growing the most revolting things they had ever seen in their lives. The moist, fleshy Worry Warts made a kind of low, grumbling sound. It was hard to tell but, when Jez looked really closely, yes, they were moving. Some of them were fat and bright purple and some of them were hairy. They had round boggly eyes in their sludge, and some of them had fat gooey lips. Some of them even had mini

THE PURPLE SLUGGY WORRY WARTS

Worry Warts growing on them. All of them were revolting.

Mr Quirk cooed at the warts as though they were kittens. Then he turned to the boys. 'If you're worrying, take a Worry Wart and apply it to your skin,' he said. 'In approximately ten seconds, it will have sucked all the worry out of you. When the Worry Wart is full of worry, simply detach it with a swift tug. Painless, simple, effective.'

'I think they're the grossest thing ever,' muttered Jez, shuddering.

'And *I* eat my own bogeys.'

Mr Quirk took an empty glass jar from a pocket in his coat, unscrewed the lid and began flicking Worry Warts into it with a gnarled yellow fingernail. Charlie swallowed hard — he thought he might be sick. When he had about twenty of the things, Mr Quirk put the lid on the jar and shoved it into Jez's hands. Jez immediately checked that the lid was on as tight as it would go. Mr Quirk opened the cupboard door and the boys tumbled out, panting and gasping for air.

'Pay now,' he snapped.

Charlie tipped the pile of change into his outstretched hand. Like Jez, he couldn't take his eyes off the repulsive purple Worry Warts, which were now squelching up the sides of the glass jar like alien slugs from the planet Puke. The boys wrinkled their noses as one of the warts suddenly sprouted a long black hair.

Mr Quirk shoved them back through the secret doorway into the emporium, muttering to himself. 'Right then. Kindly shove off,' he snarled, frogmarching them out of the door. 'You are making my emporium look shabby with your snot-nosed, gluey-fingered child-ness. It is bad for business. Goodbye. And *don't* come again.'

Jez and Charlie didn't argue. They were still mesmerized by the revolting purple sluggy Worry Warts.

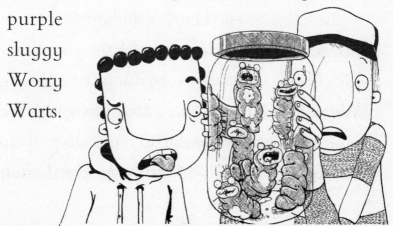

CHAPTER TWO
TOE JAM

Back in Jez's bedroom, the boys were drinking hot chocolate. They had put so many marshmallows in it, it had turned to goo.

'Let's think about this logically,' said Charlie slowly. 'We want the Box of Highly Dangerous Tricks, but Mr Quirk won't sell it to us. That's problem one.'

'I don't think that's a problem,' Jez said. 'Mr Quirk is always refusing to sell us things, but I bet he'll change his mind as soon as he smells the dosh.'

'Which brings us to problem two,' said

Charlie. 'How do we get twenty squid?'

Their brains whirred as they chewed their hot chocolate. Forty-three seconds later Jez had an idea. 'I've considered the matter carefully, and the only option is bank robbery,' he announced. 'All we need to do is shove some tights on our heads. Oh, and we'll have to disguise our voices too — bags I be Chinese.'

'Yuck!' shivered Charlie. 'I'm not putting someone's cheesy old tights on my head. Not for any money.'

'Well, at least I've thought of something,' said Jez stroppily. 'You haven't.'

Suddenly the door burst open and Francesca flounced in. She was wearing her usual twenty-eight tonnes of make-up, a bright pink silk dressing gown and pink fluffy kitten heels. But there was nothing fluffy or kitteny about her. Jez dimly remembered a time when she was his nice older sister who played Twister with him and baked him chocolate cakes. But since she'd turned thirteen she'd become absolutely vile. Mum said it was just teenage hormones that had turned her into a cross between Barbie and Godzilla, but Jez wasn't so sure. In fact, he sometimes thought his sister's body had been taken over by some kind of evil alien overlord sent from space especially to torment him.

She smiled sweetly. This made the boys extreeeeemely suspicious.

'What do you want, Francesca?' Jez demanded.

'I couldn't help hearing that you need twenty pounds,' his sister purred.

'So?'

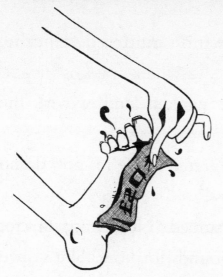

'So, I have twenty pounds.' She took off her shoe and peeled a folded note from the sweaty sole of her foot. Jez grimaced and pushed his marshmallow mush away.

'I have just heard that my beautician is ill and she can't get me ready for the talent contest at school tomorrow. I've got to look absolutely perfect, especially because Dean Best from the *Oakwood Gazette* is going to be there. He's bound to want a picture of me for the front page when I win.'

Francesca had the raving hots for Dean Best.

'*When* you win?' muttered Charlie, confused. 'But . . .'

Francesca just winked and waved the money at Jez.

'No way!' he cried. 'We're not doing beauty jobs. Gross!'

Francesca just smiled. 'No beauty jobs for me, no twenty pounds for you.' She sighed and folded the note up again. 'Oh, well, you can't have wanted it all that badly.'

Jez and Charlie looked at each other. They wanted the Box of Highly Dangerous Tricks very badly. So badly it hurt. (A lot.)

'OK, OK!' cried Jez. 'We'll do it.'

He reached out for the money, but

Francesca snatched it away.

'I'll pay you when you've finished,' she snapped. '*If* you follow my very strict instructions perfectly and without moaning, and *if* I'm fully satisfied that you two cack-handed idiots have by some miracle managed to produce results to my extremeeeely high standards.'

If Charlie and Jez had known exactly what vile tasks Francesca had in store for them, they would have put cheesy tights on their heads and robbed a bank instead.

In fact, the beauty jobs were so disgusting that, if you're about to have your tea, you should probably stop reading now.

What happened was:

1. Jez filed and painted Francesca's fingernails (bright pink, of course), while wishing Mr Quirk had sold them some Extra-Strength Fingernail Remover instead of the Worry Warts.

2. Charlie gave her a pedicure (which basically meant scraping all the stinky toe jam out from under her toenails). And she wouldn't even let him put a peg on his nose.

3. Jez plucked Francesca's eyebrows with a pair of tweezers (which he quite enjoyed doing, because it HURT).

4. Charlie flossed the bits of spinach

from last night's tea out of Francesca's teeth (meaning he also got a lovely view right up her nose).

5. Jez smoothed fake tan (Hawaiian Bronze) on to Francesca's scrawny legs.

6. Charlie cleaned out Francesca's waxy ears with (fifteen) cotton buds.

7. Jez washed and dyed Francesca's hair, then set it in rollers (and sewed extra sequins on to her pink crushed-velvet dress while she was under the hair drier, to avoid doing the job below).

8. Charlie squeezed a giant, pulsating, pus-filled spot on her chin (NO COMMENT), while wondering if the yellow goo that shot out was the same substance that Mr Quirk used to grow Worry Warts on.

All the above was made worse by the fact that Francesca practised her songs for the talent contest the whole time, and she was a seriously diabolical singer. In fact, I'm not sure you could even call it singing. It was more like the sound you'd get if you stood a honking donkey next to a car with its alarm going off.

After she'd tortured them with three rounds of 'I Am the One and Only' she went on to her other songs, which were 'I Feel Pretty' and 'I Will Always Love You'. But of course, Francesca being Francesca, she'd changed the words to 'I *am* pretty' and 'I will always love *me*'. Then she made them listen to her winner's speech and told them all the ideas she had for how she'd spend the thirty-pound prize money. Charlie didn't understand how she could be so confident of winning but then, that was typical Francesca – she was so in love with herself that she assumed everyone else was too.

At last, Francesca was completely primped and preened and gleaming clean. And she'd stopped singing, thank goodness. After she'd inspected herself in the mirror for twenty-two minutes, desperately trying to find something they hadn't done exactly right, she had to grumblingly admit that she was fully satisfied.

The boys breathed a sigh of relief as she handed Jez the twenty-pound note. Jez gave it to Charlie to take home, in case Francesca got any ideas about stealing it back.

At bedtime, Charlie tucked the money under his pillow for safekeeping, but neither he nor Jez slept very much that night. They were far too excited about buying the Box of Highly Dangerous Tricks.

CHAPTER THREE
THE BOX OF HIGHLY DANGEROUS TRICKS

Early the next morning on their way to school, Jez and Charlie took a detour down Bleak Street. Charlie had the twenty-pound note clutched in his hand. Jez knocked on the heavy oak door of Quirk's.

The door opened a crack and one dark eye examined them, then . . . SLAM!

'We've got money,' called Jez.

The door creaked open again. Mr Quirk sniffed the air. 'Phwoar! You stink!' he screeched. 'Enter.'

Grinning, they stepped inside.

'We want to buy the Box of Highly Dangerous Tricks,' said Jez boldly, as Charlie handed over the twenty-pound note.

Mr Quirk snatched the money and vanished it away into his pocket. He muttered to himself as he opened the display case and reached inside. He lifted out the Box of Highly Dangerous Tricks, tiptoed over to the big wooden desk and set it down carefully. Then, with a flick of his bony fingers, he pointed to two old chairs. As the boys sat down, clouds of dust rose up from the faded tapestry cushions.

Mr Quirk lowered himself into his frayed purple velvet armchair, knees creaking, and pulled a piece of yellow card from beneath a pile of drawing pins. The bones in his fingers crackled as he gripped his old-fashioned pen. He stared intently at it for a moment, then ink sprayed high into the air. 'It's my new invention, a *real* fountain pen full of Th-Ink,' he said proudly. The Th-Ink landed in splatters and splashes all over

the page, forming the following words:

> ## QUIRK'S,
> ### 1 BLEAK STREET.
> ### TEL: OAKWOOD 131313
>
> BOX OF HIGHLY DANGEROUS TRICKS X 1 (UNIQUE)
>
> OPEN BOX AND STAND LID ON FLAT SURFACE.
>
> QUIRK'S TAKES NO RESPONSIBILITY FOR ANY
> RESULTS OR OTHERWISE EXPERIENCED
> WHILE USING OUR PRODUCTS.
> NOR DO WE OFFER REFUNDS.

Mr Quirk wound a piece of string round and round the Box of Highly Dangerous Tricks and tied it tightly in a double knot. Then he tucked the card under the string and placed the box carefully down on Charlie's outstretched palms.

'Take care of it, boys, won't you,' he said, without his usual sharpness. He was looking at the Box of Highly Dangerous

Tricks oddly. Almost, well, fondly.

Jez and Charlie found this very strange. 'We will,' Jez assured him.

Mr Quirk held the door open and the boys stepped outside. 'Goodbye, lovely Box of Highly Dangerous Tricks,' he said wistfully. 'And goodbye, revolting brats. Oh, and don't forget to feed them.'

'Feed them?' spluttered Jez, but the solid oak door had slammed shut.

WHAT'S IN THE BOX?

At school, Jez and Charlie sat in their secret place at the back of the cloakrooms, with the Box of Highly Dangerous Tricks between them. It was safe to talk, because the bell hadn't gone yet and everyone else was still outside in the playground.

'Er, Jez, you know when Mr Quirk said "don't forget to feed them"? Well, he was joking, wasn't he?'

'I hope so,' said Jez. 'Though I don't think Mr Quirk actually *has* a sense of humour.'

'That's what I thought,' groaned Charlie as Jez opened the box.

Inside were three tiny creatures in stripy coats. They were all fast asleep. 'These aren't tricks! What a swizz!' grumbled Jez. He eyed the creatures critically. 'What are they doing in here? Maybe they sneaked in and chucked out all the actual tricks.'

In a split second, the creatures' eyes shot open and they leaped up and started pinging about, doing back flips and double-somersaults off Charlie's head and shoulders, making him laugh with delight.

'I'm Jivie!' cried the creature in the green stripy coat. 'And he's Pinkum,' he added, pointing to his friend in the red stripes. His voice was loud and strong, and seemed far too big for his body.

'And I'm Blip!' sang the one in the purple stripes. He vaulted off Charlie's ear and landed back inside the box, on the seat of a miniature drum kit, and began to play.

'We are the amazing . . .' cried Jivie.

'The astounding . . .' cried Blip.

'THE INCREDIBLY BENDY TRICKLES!' they yelled together.

The tiny drum thundered. It was like a storm in a teacup. Then it stopped suddenly, leaving an eerie silence. Charlie clapped. Jez looked unimpressed.

They had a closer look in the box and saw:

 Nine juggling balls (three green,
three purple and three red)

A magician's box

 A dangerous-looking saw

A pair of pretend feet

 Two small packets labelled
Crackle Spark Powder

A miniature drum kit

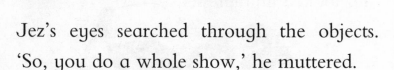 A tiny brown paper parcel

A cannon

Jez's eyes searched through the objects. 'So, you do a whole show,' he muttered.

'Yes,' replied Jivie proudly. 'We sing, dance, juggle and do the tricks. As a finale, we shoot Pinkum out of the cannon.'

'Doesn't he have a crash helmet?' asked Charlie, concerned.

'Oh, there's no need to worry about Pinkum,' Jivie assured him. 'He's got a very . . . ahem . . . hard head.'

'The cannon trick goes down ever so well at magical folks' parties,' added Blip. 'Pinkum usually manages to land in someone's cocktail.'

'Mumbalumba-looba,' muttered Pinkum. His eyes shifted about sneakily, and there was a strange grin on his face. He reached down and scratched his bottom through his red stripy suit. 'Mumbalumba-looba. Hurrumph.'

'Pinkum doesn't speak Human,' Jivie explained. 'Only Trickelese.'

'Oh, right. Is he saying nice to meet us then?' asked Jez, frowning at Pinkum.

Blip coughed. 'Ahem . . . something like that,' he replied, red-faced.

Jez peered into the Box of Highly Dangerous Tricks. 'Don't you have stilts?' he asked. 'They're my favourite.'

'No,' said Jivie regretfully. 'You see, we're very, very short and on stilts we're just a bit less short. So it's not that funny. Besides, I don't like heights.'

'Oh,' said Jez, disappointed.

'I can saw Jivie in half though,' offered Blip.

Jez finally looked impressed. 'Wow! Does it hurt?'

'Not at all,' said Jivie. 'I just poke the

pretend feet out of the end of the box and bend my knees up once I'm inside.'

'Oh,' Jez said again, with a sigh. 'The thing is, you're very nice and everything, but we bought the Box of Highly Dangerous Tricks because we thought it had tricks inside. You know, the sort that we could play on my pure-evil-in-human-form teenage sister. So you're not really what we're looking for.'

On hearing this, the Trickles slumped down as disappointed as Jez.

Then Charlie had a brainwave. 'Unless . . .' he muttered.

'Unless what?' asked Jez.

'Unless – well, what would be the ultimate trick we could play on Francesca, the one that would send her more hoppingly fizzingly mad than anything else?'

Jez felt even more annoyed. 'I don't know. Just spit it out, will you?' he said grumpily.

But he couldn't upset Charlie, whose eyes were gleaming with mischief. 'We enter the talent contest with the Trickles, as a magic act, and we beat Francesca and win the money,' he said.

Jez stared at him. Then a huge grin broke out on his face. 'Char, you are an absolute genius!' he cried.

'I thank you,' said Charlie, doing a little bow.

'So you do need us after all?' asked Jivie.

The boys nodded and the Trickles all jumped around with glee.

'We've never performed in front of non-magical people before!' cried Blip. 'They'll be amazed. We'll knock their socks off!'

So Jivie and Blip talked them through the performance as Pinkum fell back to sleep in the corner of the Box of Highly Dangerous Tricks. It was agreed that Jez and Charlie would be the assistants and announce the different tricks and set things up on a table on stage, so that the Trickles would be high enough for everyone to see. Jez felt totally sure of winning. After all, who else would have three tiny magical acrobats in their act?! They'd walk it!

'Oh, it's going to be great!' Jivie declared when they'd finished. 'It was so boring being asleep all the time at Quirk's. Performance is what we live for!'

'I can't wait for the talent contest!' cried Blip joyfully.

'Why stop at one measly talent contest?' asked Jez, beaming. 'As you said, no one from the normal world has ever seen anything like you. Let's quit school and leave home and travel all over the country doing shows. The Incredibly Bendy Trickles and The Fabulous Magic Boys! We'll be famous! How about it?'

'Erm, h-hang on a tic—' stammered Charlie.

'Great!' squealed Jivie and Blip, leaping high in the air and turning gleeful somersaults.

'Performing every day!'

'It's a dream come true!'

Jez laughed out loud. 'You guys are so much fun,' he cried.

'Er, Jez—' Charlie began.

But Jez wasn't listening. He just grabbed Charlie's wrist and checked his watch. 'Oh heck, it's nearly registration time and we still need to ask Mr Dalston if we can be in the talent competition. I hope it's not too late to enter.'

As Jez headed off to the staff room, Charlie turned to their new friends. 'OK then. I'll put the lid back on now,' he told them. 'See you later.'

'Bye-bye,' said Jivie.

Pinkum looked up
at Charlie. 'Munchum,
munchum,' he grunted.

Charlie frowned.
'What's he saying?'

'He's saying he's
hungry,' said Jivie, blushing. 'I'm sorry,
Charlie. Trickles usually wait until they're
offered food. But Pinkum's manners are
terrible.'

Charlie smiled. 'Don't worry. It's lucky
he mentioned it. We don't know anything
about looking after Trickles. What do you
eat?'

'Anything vegetable. Grass, daisies,
leaves, carrots . . . anything.'

Blip nudged him. 'But if there are peas,
then we only eat peas. Peas are the best
food on the planet.'

Charlie thought. 'Well, I don't have any peas, but we'll stop and pick some daisies on the way – how about that?'

'Daisies would be wonderful,' said Jivie gallantly.

'Mumbalumba-munchum-munch,' muttered Pinkum.

'We'd better get some sleep before the contest,' said Blip, snuggling down again.

Charlie retied the string tightly round the box, so that it didn't joggle open. He wished he could be excited like Jez, but worries were gathering in his brain like big black clouds.

Chapter Five

WORRY WARTS

'I'm not sure about all this,' said Charlie, when Jez returned from the staff room.

'About what?' Jez demanded. 'Mr Dalston says we can be in the contest, and we even get the morning off lessons to help finish the stage set. It's all good, Char.'

Charlie spoke in a low whisper, in case the Trickles had some kind of supersonic sleep-hearing. 'I mean about the Trickles. We don't really know how to look after them. And besides, what are they going to do when we're at school all day?'

Jez shrugged. 'They'll sleep in the box.

Anyway, we're not going to *be* at school, are we?'

'That's another thing,' huffed Charlie, as they made their way to the school hall. 'There's a reason they've never performed in front of non-magic people. It's obviously for their own safety. Most people don't believe in magic. If we go round showing the Trickles off everywhere, someone's bound to try and steal them, or the government will confiscate them from us and do loads of tests on them in a lab.'

But Jez didn't look bothered. 'Then we'll just say they're animatronic – you know, little robotic acrobats controlled by computers. As long as we don't let anyone actually get hold of one and examine it, they'll be fine.'

But Charlie wasn't convinced. 'Even if that worked, your parents will never let you leave school to be in a magic show—' he began.

'They can't stop me,' Jez said crossly.

'They can. And slow down, will you? I'm trying not to wobble the box. The poor Trickles are asleep.'

Jez stopped still and glared at Charlie. 'There, is that slow enough for you?' he asked sarcastically.

'Jez, don't be like that. Listen . . .'

'No, you listen!' Jez shouted. 'The Trickles are great. I want to keep them forever. I want to beat Francesca in the talent contest. I want to win the prize money. I want to be a Fabulous Magic Boy and tour the country and be famous. And that is what I'm going to do!'

'Not if I don't want to,' said Charlie quietly. 'The Trickles half belong to me.'

Jez gave a petulant sigh. 'Why do you always have to get in a stew and make things difficult?' he demanded. 'Chill out, Char. There's nothing to worry about.'

'Nothing to worry about? Yeah, right!' snorted Charlie.

That gave Jez an idea. He slipped his hand into his schoolbag and found the glass jar. He unscrewed the lid and pulled out a Worry Wart. It felt absolutely disgusting.

'The other thing is,' Charlie was saying,

'we've got to sneak out on to the playing field and pick some—'

'Yeah, whatever, mate,' said Jez, slapping Charlie on the shoulder, and secretly sticking the Worry Wart to his neck. It hung there, purple and sluggy and hairy and revolting. Charlie suddenly stopped talking.

'So, what were you saying?' Jez prompted. 'We have to pick some what?'

Charlie shrugged. 'Can't remember,' he drawled lazily. He sighed. 'It can't have been anything important.'

Wow, thought Jez. Those Worry Warts really work – and fast too! The new improved Charlie is much more chilled out.

But the new improved Charlie had already made a serious mistake. Forgetting to pick some daisies for the Trickles to eat was not 'no big deal' at all. It was, in fact, a flipping great huge deal. If only the new improved Charlie had realized that, none of the following terrible events would have happened.

CHAPTER SIX

AWFUL FRANCESCA

Mr Dalston was a portly ginger-haired man. He always wore brightly coloured ties that clashed with his brightly coloured shirts. The other contestants gradually trickled into the hall and gathered round him. Jez and Charlie knew that Francesca had entered the room without even turning around, because as soon as she caught sight of them, she screeched, 'WHAT are THEY doing HERE?!' at about five million decibels.

The boys' stomachs sank. Francesca marched across the stage, a vision of fury in pink leg warmers.

'Now, Francesca,' said Mr Dalston jovially. 'I know they are a late entry. But the show is for charity. The more the merrier, I say!'

'Well, I don't!' she stropped. 'It's not fair!'

Jez stuck out his tongue at his sister. Francesca lunged for him and dug her pink fingernails into his ribs.

'Argh!' he yelled, and tried to get her in a headlock. Farting on her head was usually his best form of self-defence.

'Now, now,' chuckled Mr Dalston, pulling them apart with his huge hands. 'It's only for fun.'

'Fun? *Fun?*' cried Francesca. 'This is the cut-throat world of show biz, darling! This is the start of my glorious career as an international pop star! I don't want those two idiots in the contest. They'll SPOIL it!'

'Don't be silly,' said Mr Dalston. 'They're in the show, Francesca, whether you like it or not.'

'Over my dead body!' screeched Francesca.

'Bonus!' said Jez with a grin. He braced himself for another attack but, to his amazement, his sister just spun on her stiletto heels and flounced off, muttering to herself.

Jez should have been suspicious about Francesca giving up that easily, but he was so excited about the contest he didn't even think about it. And of course Charlie was too deeply chilled out to notice anything at all.

Mr Dalston sighed. 'Artistic people are all the same,' he said. 'Very difficult. Don't worry, I can handle Francesca. I've already had to tell her she can only sing one song.'

'Good move,' said Jez. 'She's got a voice like ten angry alley cats trapped in a bag.'

Charlie sniggered, but Mr Dalston politely ignored this comment and explained the rules of the contest to them. 'So, you watch all the other acts and then vote for your favourite. You can't vote for yourself, obviously. The act with the most votes wins. It's just a bit of friendly fun.'

'OK,' said the boys.

'So, what's your act?' Mr Dalston asked, peering with interest at the Box of Highly Dangerous Tricks.

'It's, erm, a magic show, sort of thing,' mumbled Jez.

'Wonderful!' cried Mr Dalston in delight, clapping his hands together. 'That's just what the talent contest needs. And I can guess what's in the box.'

Charlie grinned. 'Bet you can't,' he said.

'Let's see. It's too small for a white rabbit so
. . . my guess is white mice for your tricks.'

Charlie was about to tell Mr Dalston to
guess again, but Jez nudged him hard.

'You're right,' said Jez. 'That's exactly
what they are. White mice.'

Charlie gave Jez a confused look.

'How marvellous,' said Mr Dalston. 'I'll
put them safely backstage, on top of the
cupboard, until the contest. Then you can
help with painting the backdrop.'

'OK,' said Jez.

'Whatever, dude,' said the newly relaxed
Charlie.

They followed Mr Dalston backstage. Jez
whispered to Charlie, 'If they think we've
only got mice, it'll be even more of a
surprise when everyone sees the Trickles.'

Charlie nodded. 'Good thinking,' he drawled.

They both watched Mr Dalston place the Box of Highly Dangerous Tricks carefully on top the cupboard. 'It'll be perfectly safe there,' he promised them.

CHAPTER SEVEN
THE TRICKLES
IN TROUBLE

'Let's just stop for a minute,' groaned Jez.

He and Charlie collapsed on to the stage, worn out. They had been cutting and gluing and painting and sandpapering all morning. 'Char, just go and check on the Trickles, would you?'

Charlie stretched lazily. 'Naa. You do it, man. I wanna chill.'

There were downsides to sticking the Worry Wart on Charlie, Jez decided. For one, Charlie usually did all the hard work. Now Jez was having to do it himself.

He wandered to the back of the stage and climbed on to the chair. He reached up and tilted the Box of Highly Dangerous Tricks towards him. He gasped when he saw that the string had been cut.

'Jivie? Blip?' he whispered uncertainly.

Silence.

'What? Where? How?' he gasped. 'Oh, no! No, no, no! Char, they've gone!' he cried. 'They're missing!'

'They must be in there somewhere, dude,' drawled Charlie. 'The string was done up tight.'

'Well it's not now,' hissed Jez. 'Come and look, will you?'

Charlie sighed deeply, rolled to his feet and lolloped over.

Jez pulled down the empty Box of Highly Dangerous Tricks and shoved it under Charlie's nose. 'See? They're gone!' he yelled.

Charlie shrugged. 'Don't worry, Jez. It's no big deal.'

'NO BIG DEAL?!' screeched Jez, panic stricken. 'We're  supposed to be looking after them! They're so little! They could get sat on or stepped on or shut in a door. Anything could happen! Don't you care . . . ?' Jez suddenly stopped shouting. He realized what was wrong with Charlie. He lunged at his friend and grabbed the Worry Wart from his neck. It was fat and purple with all the worry it had sucked out of Charlie, and it was still pulsating. Jez's stomach heaved and he was nearly sick.

'Ouch! What was that?' Charlie cried, then, 'OH, NO! THE TRICKLES ARE MISSING! WHAT ARE WE GOING TO DO?!'

'That's more like it,' said Jez, with relief.

'More like what?'

Jez thought he'd better own up. 'I stuck this on you to stop you worrying about everything,' he confessed, showing Charlie the fat purple sluggy Worry Wart. 'And you completely chilled out. It was brill, but now I realize I like you better just as you are. We've got to find the Trickles, and I can't do it without you. I need the old Charlie back. Do you forgive me?'

Charlie felt annoyed with Jez, but pleased too. Jez needed him. Just the way he was. 'Course I forgive you,' he said.

'Thanks, Char. OK, what do we do?'

'First, we must look for clues.' Charlie peered at the Box of Highly Dangerous Tricks. 'This string's been cut on purpose. But cut with what? Not scissors. It's frayed, as if something blunt has sawn at it. And there are these tiny pink flakes of what looks like old paint on the string.' He examined the chair seat. 'And here – two deep dents in the leather.'

Jez sighed. 'Not paint – nail polish. And dents from stiletto heels,' he said. 'That can only mean one thing.'

They looked at each other, frowning, and at the same time they both said, 'Francesca.'

She'd said she didn't want them in the contest, and now she'd made sure that they *couldn't* be in it.

Jez and Charlie raced around the school, looking for Francesca. They finally found her in the empty classroom that was being used as a changing room, individually polishing the sequins on her bright pink costume.

Jez marched right up to her. 'Where are they?' he demanded.

'I don't know what you're talking about,' his sister replied with a sly smile.

'Yes, you do,' Jez insisted. 'We saw your heel marks on the chair, so we know it was you. You've kidnapped them. Now tell me where they are.'

Francesca sighed. 'How should I know?' she snapped. 'I just opened the lid a bit—'

'Francesca!' cried Jez. 'How could you just let them loose like that? They could be in serious danger!'

Francesca rolled her eyes to the ceiling. 'Calm down, they're only mice,' she said.

'MICE?' yelped Charlie in bewilderment. 'They're not mice, they're—'

'Our special white mice,' Jez said quickly. He didn't want Francesca to know about the Trickles. 'You overheard us telling Mr Dalston about them, didn't you?'

'Yes,' said Francesca smugly. 'And now your mice are mysteriously missing. So you can't do your stupid little magic show. What a terrible tragedy.'

Jez took a swipe at her.

'Missed,' giggled Francesca, and flounced out of the room.

Charlie sniffed the air and suddenly

remembered something. 'Oh, bloomin' heck!' he gasped. 'I forgot to pick the daisies!'

'Char, that is the weirdest thing I've ever heard you say.'

Charlie remembered that Jez was outside when the Trickles had asked for food. 'I promised Jivie I'd pick some daisies for them to eat,' he gabbled. 'They were really hungry. But I completely forgot. They must be starving by now. And guess what their favourite food is . . .'

Jez blinked at him. He sniffed the air too. 'Oh no. Not peas.'

Charlie groaned. 'Yep.'

'Let's go.'

The boys raced down to the kitchen, burst through the swing doors and made a lunge for the huge pan of peas on the gas range.

'What do you think you're doing in here? Get out!' the burly cook bellowed, trying to poke them back into the dining room with a wooden spoon. 'No children allowed in the kitchen. It's health and safety rules!'

'But, Elspeth, we—'

'Out!' she shouted again.

'Can we just get—' began Charlie, stretching for the pan of peas. He gasped in horror as he caught a glimpse of a tiny purple stripy coat bobbing about in it.

'No! Now get out or I'll whisk you out.'
Elspeth grabbed her electric whisk, flicked a
switch and waved the whirring blades at

them. Jez and Charlie
were not going to
argue with that. They
stumbled back through
the doors, got tangled
together and tumbled
on to the floor.

'We need an adult to
go in there,' said Charlie, rubbing his
bruised behind.

'You're right,' sighed Jez, wiping floor
fluff off his face. 'But it has to be someone
who knows the Trickles. If someone else
gets hold of them, they might realize they're
real creatures and take them away from us.'

Charlie thought for a moment. 'Yeah,

that's true. But it also has to be someone Elspeth will let into the kitchen.'

'But that's two people,' whispered Jez. 'The only person who knows about the Trickles is Mr Quirk and the only person Elspeth will let into the kitchen is a health inspector.'

'Well then, Mr Quirk will have to pretend to be a health inspector,' said Charlie.

'He'll never agree,' said Jez.

'Jez, it's our only hope. They're in there. I saw a bit of one. They're in deadly danger. I've still got the Box of Highly Dangerous Tricks' instruction card in my pocket, with his phone number on. I'll grab my mobile and call him this second.'

'No, I'll do it,' said Jez firmly. 'If I hadn't put that Worry Wart on you, you would have remembered the daisies and the

Trickles would have been full up and they would have stayed in the box and they wouldn't be in the kitchen getting boiled up or stamped on or skewered or worse. It's my fault we're in this mess.'

'It's Francesca's fault we're in this mess,' Charlie told him firmly. 'But make the call if you like. I don't fancy being on the receiving end when Mr Quirk finds out what's happened to the Trickles.'

Jez gulped. He didn't fancy it either. Not one little bit.

Needless to say, the phone call did not go well.

'Is he coming?' Charlie asked.

Jez shook his head. 'He says it's our mess and we have to sort it out. Well, he didn't say it as politely as that – there was a lot more swearing.'

As the dining room filled up with kids, they both stared miserably through the porthole glass in the kitchen doors. Then suddenly they felt hands clapping down on their shoulders. They looked up to find Mr Dalston grinning at them. 'Don't look so glum, boys. It can't be that bad.'

'It is,' groaned Jez. Any minute now the Trickles would be served up. He knew that they had no option but to come clean about them. Well, clean-ish. He wouldn't mention that they were real magic creatures. 'You see . . .'

Just then, the fire door burst open. In strode Mr Quirk, his rickety knees creaking. He was wearing a black bowler hat and he had a bulbous fake nose and a bristly moustache stuck to his face. He was clutching a briefcase in his bony hand. His

dark eyes flashed furiously behind thick spectacles.

Jez and Charlie dashed over to him. 'You came!'

Mr Quirk gave them a furious glare. 'I only changed my mind because I was concerned about the Trickles!' he hissed. 'I'm not here to help you two! You incompetent idiots! You numbskulled nincompoops! You –' Then he seemed to remember why he was there, snarled, 'I'll deal with you later,' and addressed Mr Dalston. 'I am the health inspector,' he announced in a strange nasal voice. 'I have had a report that there are rodents loose in this building. This is a very serious matter. If they are not found, I'll have to close the school right now.'

'But that's out of the question,' Mr

Dalston insisted. 'We have a talent contest this afternoon. It can't be cancelled. I assure you there are no rodents here.'

'But, Mr Dalston, that's what we were about to tell you,' lied Jez. 'The white mice for our magic show – they've escaped.'

The smile fell right off Mr Dalston's face. 'Well, in that case, you'd better find them . . . and quickly!'

'I shall begin inspecting the building at once, starting with the kitchen,' said Mr Quirk curtly. 'And these two blundering ninkazoids can help me identify the offending vermin.'

CHAPTER EIGHT
PEA PROBLEMS

'I demand to come in!' bellowed Mr Quirk masterfully.

Elspeth the cook finished shoving a white china tureen and a tray of pork chops through the serving hatch and marched to the doorway. There she stood with her powerful hands on her ample hips, staring at Mr Quirk with utter contempt. 'WHAT?' she boomed.

Mr Quirk gulped. 'I demand to come in,' he repeated timidly.

'Not on your Nelly!' Elspeth bellowed, her face flushing red with fury.

'Who's Nelly?' asked Jez.

'Not now!' hissed Charlie.

Elspeth's face went redder and redder until she looked positively volcanic. 'There's nothing wrong with my kitchen! Go away!'

'Please, Elspeth,' Jez begged. 'The inspector only wants a little look. It won't take a minute. We've lost our white mice.'

'Not on your Nigel!'

Elspeth's muscle-bound arms twitched, causing Mr Quirk to shudder in his shabby shoes. He could hear the sound of feet scuffling down the stairs. It was now or never. 'I must come in this very minute!' he insisted.

'Not on your Nicholas Nathaniel Norbert!' roared Elspeth. 'And that's my last name on the subject.'

Mr Quirk shook the terrible thoughts from his head and summoned all his courage. 'Let me in now!' he shouted suddenly, squaring up to the cook. 'NOW, I say, or I shall fail it all! I'll fail, fail, fail the whole dashed lot!' He waggled a bony finger menacingly at her. 'You'll have cooked your last lunch!'

Elspeth was furious, but she realized she had no choice. 'I'm going to complain to the headmaster about this!' she fumed, marching out of the kitchen.

Charlie and Jez ran round to the dining room and leaned through the hatch.

'The peas, Mr Quirk,' called Jez.

Mr Quirk whirled around and whipped the lid off the pea pan. 'Gadzooks!' he cried.

Something was making the peas move about.

Mr Quirk stirred them around. He lifted up big scoops and threw them down again, muttering. Suddenly he stopped, holding the spoon in mid-air.

Sitting on a scoop of slippery peas, trying not to slide off, was Jivie. 'Mr Quirk! What an unexpected pleasure,' he cried.

Mr Quirk plucked Jivie from the spoon

and plonked him on the edge of the pan.

Jivie gasped for breath, then burped delicately. 'Oh, do excuse me! If I eat another pea, I'll pop!'

Then two purple stripy arms appeared. Blip hauled himself on to the spoon, panting hard. 'Oh, quick, quick, Mr Quirk!' he gabbled, frantic with worry. 'Pinkum's gone! He's been served up! We've got to—'

Before Blip could say 'save him', Mr Quirk had stuffed him into his left pocket. He shoved Jivie into his right and stalked out of the kitchen. On the way round to the dining room he banged straight into Elspeth.

'Have you finished meddling? Can I go back into my own kitchen now?' she asked with a sneer.

'I beg your pardon?' mumbled Mr Quirk, rubbing his head.

'The inspection,' said Elspeth, peering at him suspiciously.

'Er . . . oh, yes. Pass. Pass. It all passes.'

Elspeth watched the 'health inspector' stumble off into the dining room. 'There's something not right with that one,' she muttered.

Three and a half seconds later, Mr Quirk was stopped in his tracks in the doorway by a sight so horrible, so vile, it would put you off your dinner.

About two hundred kids sat at long tables. Knives and forks clashed and scraped on plates, above a steady chorus of chomping. Mr Quirk could tell what they were eating without even looking at the plates, because so many of the children were talking with their mouths full. Food-spit was spraying everywhere. Plastic cups were knocked over and water spilt.

Mr Quirk looked at the green goo that was globbing round the children's mouths like sopping sheets in a washing machine. 'I hope it's not too late,' he muttered. Jez and Charlie exchanged a terrified look.

'Keep out of sight,' Mr Quirk whispered to Jivie and Blip. 'We're going in.'

He hovered by one of the huge long tables. He spotted the white china tureen he had seen Elspeth shove through the serving hatch. One of the lunch monitors was serving up peas from it. She'd done a whole table already.

Mr Quirk rolled up the sleeves of his pinstriped jacket and waded in. 'Don't be alarmed!' he called. 'I'm a health inspector! My assistants and I are required to inspect your lunches. Heads back, mouths open. Do NOT swallow whatever you've got in there!'

The kids stared at him, completely bewildered. But they didn't dare move a millimetre.

'This is ridiculous!' Francesca muttered to Jacintha Arbuthnot-Smythe and Claudia Banshee, her two best (and only) friends. 'And typical of my creepy brother to volunteer as a helper. Still, we'd better do it. That health inspector looks deranged.'

All three girls opened their mouths.

Mr Quirk looked into theirs and every other open mouth at that table and shuddered. There was a greasy green mush in every moosh.

'Pass . . . pass . . . pass . . .' he chanted as he inspected the contents of each mouth and saw no Pinkum.

Charlie and Jez did the same, calling out 'pass . . . pass . . . pass' as they went.

Now that Mr Quirk had moved away from her, Francesca felt annoyed about the inspection. She didn't like being told what to do. Idly, she picked up a pea and threw it across the room.

And that single pea started the biggest pea fight in the history of pea fights ever (and, yes, that does include the infamous Green Friday fight that took place in Berlin in 1782, before you ask).

Round green bullets shot through the air. Children were ducking to avoid them and leaping on to their chairs to get a clear shot. There was screaming and screeching.

Mr Dalston was shouting himself hoarse, but no one heard him.

Mr Quirk's dark eyes flashed around the room. He'd had quite enough. All the pea throwing was making it impossible to inspect the lunches.

'STOP THE MADNESS!' he yelled.

There was a stunned silence. Hands hovered with unthrown peas in them. Everyone, including Mr Dalston, stared at Mr Quirk, their mouths hanging open.

Justin Faraday's mouth hung open just long enough for Pinkum to wake up and realize that he was in it. He slid off Justin's tongue, down his tie and on to his plate. He pulled a pork chop over himself and ran for it.

By this time, Mr Quirk was absolutely incandescent with fury, which kind of means that he was so mad he was almost on fire. 'HOW CAN I INSPECT THE LUNCHES WHEN THEY ARE FLYING AROUND THE ROOM!' he bellowed.

The stunned silence continued. Everyone stared at Mr Quirk. No one moved a muscle. Then, 'AAAAAAAAHHHHHHH!' screamed Francesca. She leaped a metre in the air and landed on the table. Justin Faraday's pork chop was dashing past her feet, dodging cups and plates.

'Hurrumph! Hurrumph! Hurrumph! Hurrumph!' it went.

'It's alive!' Francesca shrieked.

Suddenly Elspeth strode in through the dining room door. 'It's not alive, you soft girl!' she bellowed. 'There's just a mouse under it.'

Francesca screamed.

Elspeth had the electric whisk in her hand.

'Don't worry, Mr Dalston, I'll get the little blighter!' she bellowed. She pushed a button and the electric whisk started up. The two blades whirred round at eighty-four miles an hour.

Jez gasped. Pinkum wouldn't stand a chance against such a lethal weapon. Elspeth stood in wait at the end of Francesca's table, a terrible leering grin on her face. The pork chop was running straight towards the flashing metal.

Knees creaking, Mr Quirk bolted across the room and threw himself on to the table. He grabbed the pork chop and hurled it into the air. But Pinkum was still running, eyes squeezed shut and arms outstretched, straight at the whizzing blades.

'That's not a mouse!' cried Tabitha Bell. 'It's a strange little something!'

Everyone looked and everyone gasped.

Lightning fast, Jez ran and dived between the whisk and Pinkum. Just as Pinkum was about to hit the deadly blades, he scooped him up to safety. 'Save!' he shouted.

The children burst into applause. Then they started muttering and pointing. They had never seen anything like Pinkum before.

Pinkum was squirming like an eel, but Jez managed to stuff him into Mr Quirk's left pocket. Blip grabbed him and held a hand over his mouth.

Jez and Charlie grinned at each other. They'd done it! All the Trickles were safe and the show could go on!

Everything was going to be fine.

'RIGHT . . .' began Mr Quirk.

Mr Dalston and the children turned and gaped in surprise. Jez gasped and Charlie groaned. Mr Quirk's disguise had slipped. His false nose was hanging off and his long,

 pointy real nose had sprung out from underneath it. His moustache hung limply down one side of his mouth.

Everything was *not* going to be fine.

CHAPTER NINE
MR QUIRK UNCOVERED

'IMPOSTER!' shrieked Elspeth.

In panic, Mr Quirk bolted across the dining room, but the angry cook blocked the doorway. She pointed the whisk at him and revved it menacingly. 'I knew something weren't right with you,' she crowed.

The children began to whisper to one another in amazement. Mr Dalston just stared at Mr Quirk in disbelief.

'Call the police, Mr Dalston,' Elspeth ordered.

'No, wait! I can explain!' All eyes swung from Mr Quirk to Jez.

'He means, we can explain,' added Charlie.

'I hope you can, boys,' said Mr Dalston sternly.

'This is Mr Quirk,' said Jez. 'He's not a health inspector, he's a shopkeeper.'

'Emporium proprietor,' corrected Mr Quirk crossly. He winced as he ripped the false moustache off his face. The children stared as he removed the horn-rimmed spectacles and the bulbous fake nose.

'And inventions genius,' added Charlie, hoping to butter him up. But Mr Quirk just gave him an evil glare.

Mr Dalston looked even more confused. 'Does this fiasco have anything to do with your magic show?' he asked the boys.

Jez nodded.

Just then a few of the children gasped and pointed to Mr Quirk's pinstripe jacket. Tiny hands sticking out from purple and green stripy sleeves were clutching on to the pocket tops. Everyone was staring now as Jivie and Blip tried to heave themselves out. Then, 'Ouch!' they squealed, as Mr Quirk poked them back down with his long bony fingers.

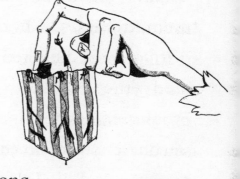

'They're not mice!' exclaimed Mr Dalston. 'But what on earth are they?'

Alarmed, Mr Quirk looked at Jez, and Jez looked at Charlie, and Charlie realized there was no one else to look at so he did some split-second thinking. 'As I said, Mr

Quirk is a genius inventor,' he began. 'Well, actually, he specializes in computers.'

Everyone looked at Mr Quirk, surprised.

He looked like he'd never switched on a computer in his life, which indeed he hadn't. 'He works mainly in the field of animatronics,' Charlie blundered on, getting more flustered by the second. 'He used the world's most sophisticated programming techniques and the latest silicone engineering to create these robotic creatures called Trickles. That's why we were so desperate to get them back. They're prototypes and they're completely priceless.'

Mr Quirk and Charlie and Jez all held their breath. Surely there was no way Mr Dalston would believe that? But, amazingly, he did. After all, the only alternative, that they were real live magical creatures unknown to science or nature, was absolutely impossible. So Charlie *had* to be telling the truth, didn't he?

'The Trickles can still do the show, can't they?' asked Mr Dalston hopefully.

'No, they can not!' snapped Mr Quirk. 'These boys have been utterly irresponsible. The Trickles could have died, you know. I mean, erm, been *destroyed*. Now, if you'll excuse me . . .' Mr Quirk nodded curtly to Mr Dalston and stalked towards the door.

'Oh no, don't go! We want to see the Trickles perform!' Laurence Craven's cry rang out across the silent dining room.

There was a lot of whispering and nodding among the children.

'No with knobs on!' snapped Mr Quirk.

The children looked so disappointed.

Mr Dalston was frowning too.

'Oh, Mr Quirk, please let us do the show,' cried the right pinstripe pocket.

'No with raspberry jam!' screeched Mr Quirk.

'Oh please, we really want to perform,' begged the left pocket.

'No – with a jacuzzi, a sports car and a holiday to Barbados!'

Francesca was overjoyed. 'You're out of the show, bro,' she said gleefully. 'Bad luck.'

Jez stared at the floor, feeling wretched. Francesca was right. They wouldn't get to perform with the Trickles. Or win. Or see her spontaneously combust with fury. All that toe gunk scraping for nothing! From the look on Charlie's face (that of a seasick halibut), Jez knew he was feeling just as miserable. Then he had an idea. He turned to Mr Quirk. 'If we win, we'll give you one third of the prize money,' he offered.

Mr Quirk still looked furious, but his nose twitched, so they knew he was at least thinking about it. 'Half,' he said.

Jez shrugged. 'OK, deal.'

A great cheer filled the dining room. Francesca looked extremely cross. Mr Dalston chuckled and clapped his hands together. 'Right, everyone, let's get into the dressing rooms and put on the glitz. The show starts in half an hour! And you boys can be the grand finale.'

'Hang on, you said *I* could be the finale!' Francesca whined, but Mr Dalston either didn't hear or didn't take any notice. Instead he just nodded to Mr Quirk and headed for the door. But Elspeth was still blocking the doorway, and she was still fuming.

'Everything all right, Elspeth?' Mr Dalston asked sweetly.

'No, everything is NOT all right!' bellowed the cook. 'Who's going to pick up all those peas? Waste of good food, that's what it is!'

'Quite right,' agreed Mr Dalston. 'OK, who's going to clear up this mess?' He turned and looked meaningfully at the two boys.

'Erm, I think we are . . .' sighed Charlie.

As everyone else hurried back up to the

hall, Elspeth handed Jez and Charlie a broom each. Then she marched off into the kitchen, muttering crossly to herself.

As Francesca sashayed past, Jez couldn't resist having a little dig. 'We're back in the running now, sister dear,' he said smugly. 'And we're going to win!'

To his surprise, she smiled. 'Oh, you think so, do you?' she said, cool as strawberry ice cream. 'Well, that goes to show how little you know.'

'What do you mean?' asked Charlie suspiciously.

Francesca did one of her annoying smiles.

'Let's just say I've had a little chat with the others.'

'What kind of little chat?' hissed Jez.

'Oh, you know. The kind where I order them to vote for me or else bad happenings will occur. Unfortunate Accidents. Unexpected Emergencies. That sort of thing.'

Jez and Charlie gasped. So she'd threatened the other contestants! That's why she'd been so confident about winning!

Charlie looked her straight in the eye. 'We'll stop you, Francesca,' he promised.

Francesca snorted with laughter. 'You won't! The other kids are scared stiff. Even if you tell Mr Dalston, they'll never back you up. Now, do excuse me, I need to practise my look of elated surprise for when the winner is announced.' Blowing them a little kiss, she flounced out of the room.

Charlie groaned. 'I can't believe we've got stuck here clearing up. Just when we need to get upstairs and tie your evil sister to a chair or something.'

CHAPTER TEN
BREAK A LEG

An hour later, Jez peered out from behind the stage curtain. The auditorium was filling up with excited pupils, friends and relatives, including his parents, and Charlie's mum and nan. They heard Francesca squeal, 'Dean Best's here!' and watched her check her make-up for the gazillionth time.

'Come on, boys, it's time for the circle of power,' called Mr Dalston. They joined the group of performers, but all the other children looked pale and frightened. 'There's no need to be nervous,' said Mr

Dalston soothingly, thinking they had stage fright. Only Jez and Charlie knew that they were actually terrified of Francesca and the awful threats she'd made. Jez just knew he had to stop her, and right then, at the very last second, he thought of a plan. He snuck his hand into his bag and pulled out his secret weapon. 'I would just like to tell you all to break a leg,' he announced.

Now, you may think that telling people to snap limbs isn't very nice, but that's what they say for good luck in the theatre.

Jez took Sophie Butler's hand and shook it. 'Break a leg,' he said, and then did the same to everybody else, one by one, except for Francesca, of course.

'OK, very good, well done,' said Mr Dalston impatiently. 'Now, let's get on with the circle of power.'

The circle of power was one of his special theatrical things. Everyone huddled together and jumped up and down, to pump up their energy ready for the performance.

Charlie found himself next to Francesca, who was in her full regalia, wearing her pink crushed velvet dress and matching feather boa. She had a sparkly tiara on her head.

As they huddled, Francesca

dug her pointy pink fingernails into Charlie's back.

As they jumped, she landed on his foot with her sharp stilettos.

'Argh!' he cried.

'They're all still voting for me,' she hissed into his ear. 'It's too late to stop me now!'

Charlie winced with pain. There was nothing he could say to Francesca that wouldn't involve swearing in front of a teacher, so he said nothing.

Francesca gave him a very smug look indeed.

The circle jumped higher and higher and higher. 'Go! Go! Go!' shouted Mr Dalston. When the huddle broke up, everyone was gasping for breath.

'Now, get out there and enjoy yourselves,' said Mr Dalston, grinning. 'And remember to watch the other acts from the wings, and give me your votes at the end. OK, places, everyone . . . and break a leg!'

The talent contest was brilliant. Sophie played an amazing piece on the piano with loads of twiddly bits. Laurence burped the alphabet, which was less musical, but strangely fascinating to watch. Francesca's witch friends Jacintha Arbuthnot-Smythe and Claudia Banshee did a cheerleading display which even Charlie had to admit was pretty good. Gwyn Paige and Freddie

Albrow did a comedy routine that involved hitting each other with a large rubber banana and falling over a lot, which was both funny ha ha and funny weird. And Justin Faraday ate twenty-seven cream crackers in one minute, making his mother very proud.

There were lots of other superb acts. In fact, there were far too many to mention here, so just use your imagination, OK?

Near the end of the show, Francesca strutted onstage. She had chosen to sing 'I Feel Pretty', the song with the screechiest screechy bits of all. She started belting it out, and because she had a microphone it was ten times worse than usual.

Some of the audience members and the whole cast put their fingers in their ears. Babies started bawling. Quite a few people decided they urgently needed the toilet and left the room. Mr and Mrs Lloyd sat politely through it, although they winced every time their daughter hit a high note.

By the end of the second verse, Mr Dalston had turned the microphone down so low and the music up so high that Francesca was drowned out. So she stopped singing and started yelling, 'Turn me up, you idiot! No one can hear my beautiful voice!'

Reluctantly, Mr Dalston turned the microphone up again. Three people hid under their seats. The smart man next to Dean Best grimaced, then tugged his top hat down over his ears and was soon smiling again.

When Francesca finished at last, there was only a smattering of applause. But she insisted on taking three bows anyway. Then the curtains closed so that Mr Quirk could set up the stage for the Trickles' act.

Mr Dalston appeared and threw his hands up frantically. 'You should be in your stage clothes by now, boys!' he hissed, frowning. 'Hurry! It's curtain up in one minute.'

Jez and Charlie looked at each other, then down at their paint-smeared, dust-covered jeans and T-shirts. What stage clothes?

Chapter Eleven
THE INCREDIBLY BENDY TRICKLES

Jez and Charlie stumbled on to the stage.
There behind the blue velvet curtains stood
Mr Quirk. He looked like his usual smart if
dusty self and was back in his tweed suit,
and a black cloak, with his wiry hair
frizzling out all over his head.

Mr Quirk was positioning the contents
of the Box of Highly Dangerous Tricks
carefully on a long table. The Trickles were
also on the table, doing warm ups.
This involved things like wrapping their
ankles around their necks and touching

their toes with their ears.

'Jivie! Blip! We can't do the act!' gasped Jez. 'We haven't got any stage clothes.'

'Don't panic,' said Jivie. 'Costumes are provided. Here.' He held out the tiny brown paper parcel.

Charlie took it between his fingers and thumbs, opened it and pulled out two miniature dinner suits and two teeny-weeny top hats.

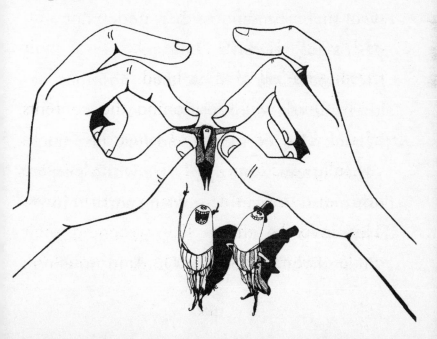

'Thirty seconds!' called Mr Dalston.

'But these are way too small,' Jez cried hysterically.

'One size fits all,' said Jivie. 'Just add water.'

Charlie grabbed the vase of flowers off the piano and tipped a little bit of water on to the suits. They grew to the perfect size straight away. The boys hurriedly put them on, scared that the curtain would go up and reveal them standing in their underpants.

'Let's go!' cried Mr Dalston.

Jez and Charlie took their positions at either side of the long table.

'Break a leg, everyone,' said Jivie, beaming.

The curtain went up. There was a purple flash and a shower of golden sparks rained down on to the stage.

A spotlight bathed Mr Quirk in an eerie

green glow. It made him look very imposing and spooky, which he rather liked. The atmosphere was electric. He cleared his throat.

'May I present our grand finale. Please welcome . . . the Fabulous Magic Boys and the amazing, the astounding, the Incredibly Bendy . . . TRICKLES!'

The audience clapped and cheered.

A bright spotlight fell on to the long table. The audience gasped in amazement when they saw the Trickles.

First Pinkum did a drum roll while Jivie and Blip performed stomach-churning acrobatics. Next, Jez and Charlie break danced while Jivie and Blip used their feet, shoulders and even noses as launch pads.

The captivated audience oohed and ahhed as Jivie and Blip flicked and flacked. Each move was more daring than the last. To finish, Jivie did a triple backwards knee-

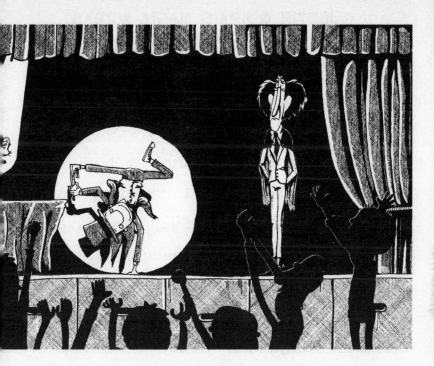

flailing twister and landed on his nose, while Blip performed a flying elbow flop with no less than four flippety-jerks. Then they vaulted into the air and came to rest on the tips of Jez's little fingers. The crowd went wild.

The acrobatics were followed by gasps of delight for the synchronized ear juggling. Then there was nail-biting tension as Charlie locked Jivie into the magician's box and Jez sawed right through him. Blood gushed out, and Jez and Charlie acted like something had gone terribly wrong. Jivie staggered round, still wearing the box, while blood spurted in every direction, before dropping dead on the table. (The audience erupted into relieved applause when he sprang up and took a bow!)

After all the pea eating at lunchtime, Pinkum nearly didn't fit into the cannon for the grand finale. But with a lot of breathing in and squishing and squeezing, Charlie and Jez managed to stuff him down the barrel and light the fuse.

BANG!

Pinkum exploded into

the air. He landed
on the shoulder
of Mr Michaels
in the third row
back. There was a

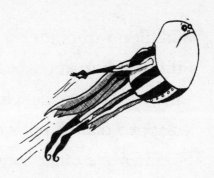

lot of cheering and clapping
as Jez returned Pinkum to the stage. The
Trickles took a bow, then another and
another, as waves of applause rolled over
them.

Finally, Jez and Charlie tore the tops off
the packets of Crackle-Spark Powder and
threw it into the audience. There were
screams of delight as rainbow firecrackers
exploded above their heads.

The applause was so loud it almost took
the roof off. The Trickles featuring the
Fabulous Magic Boys had brought the
house down! The audience had never seen

anything so amazing. The smart man with the top hat stood up and shouted, 'Bravo! Bravo!' Everyone else stood up too, and clapped and clapped and clapped.

Then the other contestants came back on stage and bowed and bowed to huge applause. Even in that glorious moment, Charlie had a dark thought, which was that he wished they could have stopped Francesca from cheating. Then they'd at least have had a chance at the thirty-pound prize. Oh well.

When the curtain fell for the last time, the performers went up to Mr Dalston and whispered the name of the act they wanted to vote for. Charlie opted for the bizarre comedy sketch and Jez went for the burping. Mr Dalston wrote each vote down on a piece of paper then counted them up.

He gathered the children around him and gave the signal for the curtain to rise again.

'Ladies and gentlemen,' he called, beaming. 'I'm sure you will agree that all the acts here today were fabulous. We've had such fun, which is the most important thing. But in every contest there must be a winner, and that winner is—'

'Wow!' squealed Francesca, dashing up to Mr Dalston, hands outstretched for the prize money. 'This is completely unexpected, but I am delighted –' She stopped abruptly. The audience stared at her in astonishment. She'd just realized that Mr Dalston hadn't said her name yet. She abandoned her speech, pulled on a forced smile and tried to look innocent.

'Francesca, what's going on?' said Mr Dalston, confused. 'You're not the winner.'

For a few seconds Francesca went such a deep shade of purple that Jez and Charlie thought she'd implode. She could still have got away with it, but she couldn't hold her anger in. She turned on the other kids. 'You little toe rags!' she screeched. 'You all promised to vote for me! Oh, you are in such deep trouble now. Prepare for UNFORTUNATE ACCIDENTS and UNEXPECTED EMERGENCIES!!!'

The audience began muttering crossly, but the children weren't frightened at all. This surprised Charlie at first, but he took one look at Jez's grin and suddenly understood what he'd done with the rest of the Worry Warts. He slapped Jez's hand in a high five.

Dean Best took a picture of Francesca's screwed-up angry puce face (complete with bulbously bulging eyes) and scribbled on his

notepad: 'Talent Contest Cheat Thwarted'.

Mr Lloyd dragged Francesca off, kicking and screaming. 'I can assure you we take cheating very seriously in our family,' he told the audience, over his shoulder.

'Yes, we do,' said Jez loudly, and Francesca gave him the most malicious look she'd ever mustered up. As Mr Lloyd wrestled her out of the hall doors, he could be heard muttering, '. . . dealt with fully . . . grounded . . . chores . . . no make-up money . . .'

This was an even more satisfying ending for Francesca than Jez or Charlie could ever have hoped for. Not only had she been found out, but she'd also been shown up, in front of everybody, including Dean Best. Who was then going to broadcast her cheating ways to the entire town. It was revenge beyond Jez's wildest dreams!

'Anyway,' said Mr Dalston, 'enough of this drama – back to the main event. I am delighted to announce that the winners are the Fabulous Magic Boys and the Amazing, the Astounding, the Incredibly Bendy TRICKLES!'

Jivie, Blip and Pinkum back flipped themselves on to the stage to join Charlie and Jez. The audience exploded into clapping and cheering once more. Jez and Charlie high-fived again, then both shook

Mr Dalston's hand and with a grin Jez accepted the prize money and went to give Mr Quirk his half.

But Charlie couldn't feel completely happy. He had something else on his mind. Something that even a whole jar of Worry Warts couldn't fix.

CHAPTER TWELVE
JEREMY FLAXENBY AND MAGIC MANSION

The audience began to file out of the hall, talking excitedly. Mr Quirk was grinning as he packed everything back into the Box of Highly Dangerous Tricks. The Trickles leaped around, chattering gleefully.

It seemed that everyone was happy except Charlie. Miserably, he shuffled back on to the stage.

'Oh, Charlie, it was wonderful!' cried Jivie. 'We were born to perform, not spend our lives asleep in a dusty old shop! With you and Jez as the Fabulous Magic Boys we can travel all round the country doing our show. It'll be fantastic. We can start on Monday.'

'I don't think so,' said Mrs Lloyd, who'd come up to congratulate them and overheard. Then she spotted a friend and hurried off, but they didn't bother to go after her. They knew that there was no point arguing. Mrs Lloyd never let Jez off school, even if he was virtually dead with a virulent lurgy. And Charlie knew his mum wouldn't let him go travelling either.

'Sorry, but we can't be Fabulous Magic Boys,' Charlie told Jivie.

'In fact, we can't keep you at all,' mumbled Jez.

Jivie and Blip were terribly upset, though they tried to hide it. Pinkum probably would have been upset too, if he hadn't been fast asleep inside the box.

'In that case, you'll have to come back to the emporium,' Mr Quirk told them.

'Oh, but we want to perform!' cried Blip despairingly.

'I'm sorry, but there's no other way,' said Mr Quirk with regret.

A loud cough behind them made them all jump. It was the smart man in the bow tie and top hat. The one who'd shouted 'Bravo!'

'Forgive me, but I couldn't help over-hearing,' he said. 'I may be able to help you with your dilemma.'

'Who are you?' asked Mr Quirk, clutching the Box of Highly Dangerous Tricks protectively.

'I am Jeremy Flaxenby,' he said. 'Delighted to meet you.'

Mr Quirk went pale. '*The* Jeremy Flaxenby?' he stuttered. 'You mean,

Jeremy Flaxenby the world-famous magician?'

'The very same,' said the man, smiling bashfully. He whipped off his top hat and pulled out a bunch of flowers to prove it. Then he handed one bloom to Jivie and Blip.

'Thank you,' they said. 'Yum yum.'

'I was very impressed with your act,' he told them. 'So impressed in fact that I would like you to come and live at Magic Mansion, and perform in my show every evening.'

'Wow! Brilliant!' cried Jivie.

'Oh please, Mr Quirk, say we can go!' Blip begged.

Mr Quirk frowned. 'No, no, no,' he muttered. 'And in case that isn't clear, NO.'

'But the Trickles belong to us,' said Jez. 'We bought them. And we want Jeremy to have them.'

Mr Quirk gave them the kind of look that would melt glass, but there was nothing he could do. Jez took the Box of Highly Dangerous Tricks from Mr Quirk and gave it to Jeremy Flaxenby.

Jivie and Blip cheered.

'You must come and visit us,' Blip told Charlie and Jez. 'We'll miss you.'

'We'll miss you too,' Charlie assured them. 'But Magic Mansion! How exciting!'

'We'll definitely come and visit!' promised Jez.

Jivie and Blip said goodbye and hugged Jez and Charlie's fingers.

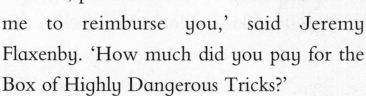

'Now, please allow me to reimburse you,' said Jeremy Flaxenby. 'How much did you pay for the Box of Highly Dangerous Tricks?'

'Twenty pounds,' said Jez. 'But don't worry about that. We're just glad they've found a good home.'

'Oh no, I insist,' said the eminent magician. He reached behind his ear, plucked out a twenty-pound note and handed it to Jez.

Then he bowed once more and strode away.

Mr Quirk turned on the boys. 'And as for you two twalloping twitbags, if you ever come near my emporium again, I'll spray you with Violent Violet Ear-Vomiting Elixir,' he hissed. Then he stalked off as fast as his creaking knees would allow.

Charlie and Jez winced. *Ear Vomit?*

Charlie snorted crossly. 'You know, he's so rude I hope I never see him again as long as I live,' he declared. 'In fact, I've decided. I'm never going back to that dusty old place ever again. Never. Ever. Definitely not.'

'Sure,' said Jez, with a sly grin, 'of course. Anything you say, mate. On the other hand, we've just made ourselves thirty-five quid. Now, I wonder what kind of wicked tricks we could get for that?'

Charlie couldn't help wondering either. Just a little bit . . .

MAKE YOUR OWN MAGIC POTIONS!

Quentin Quirk's Bouncy Bashable Brew

This bashable brew
Is as bouncy as rubber,
Except when it's not;
Then it's soupy as flubber
This peculiar potion
Is not what it seems,
First liquid, then solid
It's a physicist's dream!

You'll need:

200 g custard powder
A mixing bowl
100 ml water
A spoon
A potato masher

Pour the custard powder into the bowl and add the water. Mix with the spoon until the mixture is smooth and thick.

If you rest the potato masher on top of the mixture, it will sink. If you bash the liquid instead, the masher will bounce back!

This amazing stuff works even better when you have loads of it – if you filled a swimming pool with this loony liquid, you could run across it!

QUENTIN QUIRK'S MAGIC WORKS

ATTACK OF THE BUM-BITING SHARKS

Jez's big sister is extreeeeemely annoying. So Jez and his friend Charlie plan revenge – with a potion from local magic maker Quentin Quirk. Prepare for something snappy, toothy and very scary!

A selected list of titles available from Macmillan Children's Books

The prices shown below are correct at the time of going to press. However, Macmillan Publishers reserves the right to show new retail prices on covers, which may differ from those previously advertised.

Matt Kain

Quentin Quirk's Magic Works: Attack of the Bum-Biting Sharks!	978-0-330-51021-9	£4.99

Jo Foster

History Spies: Back to the Blitz	978-0-330-44899-4	£4.99
History Spies: Escape from Vesuvius	978-0-330-44900-7	£4.99

All Pan Macmillan titles can be ordered from our website, www.panmacmillan.com, or from your local bookshop and are also available by post from:

Bookpost, PO Box 29, Douglas, Isle of Man IM99 1BQ
Credit cards accepted. For details:
Telephone: 01624 677237
Fax: 01624 670 923
Email: bookshop@enterprise.net
www.bookpost.co.uk

Free postage and packing in the United Kingdom